The woman, five-foot-two at the most, probably weighed less than the tool she carried. He gave her the once-over. Despite her diminutive height, her body was one luscious curve after another. He blinked and let go of the curtain's edge, only to lift it a second time.

Long blonde hair cascaded across her slim shoulders, landing just above her narrow waist. Her hips flared out nicely, a shapely counter balance to her perfectly-rounded breasts.

His body stirred unexpectedly, but he dismissed the reaction as a regular early-morning occurrence. He let the curtain drop again. For all of five seconds.

Cursing his weakness for nicely built women, he pushed the heavy material aside for the third time. While he'd been doing his semi-best to ignore her, she'd made her way to the middle of the massive yard. Placing the pointed end of the wooden stake on the ground, she raised the hammer in the air and dropped the heavy steel head down firmly against the top of the stake. She repeated the hammering process another two times until the sign stood by itself.

Bewitched Day Care:
A Magical Place for Your Child

Cute slogan. The creative adman side of his brain acknowledged the catchy phrasing. Yet, all the practical side could see were the two words…day and care. Visions of screaming kids filled his thoughts, aggravating an already pounding head.

Mental note number two: move to the back bedroom, away from the street.

Bewitched

by

Nancy Fraser

Bewitched

Cover Art by *Debbie Taylor*

The Wild Rose Press, Inc.
PO Box 708
Adams Basin, NY 14410-0708
Visit us at www.thewildrosepress.com

Publishing History
First Vintage Rose Edition, 2016
Digital ISBN 978-1-5092-0971-2
Print ISBN 978-1-5092-1180-7

Published in the United States of America

Dedication

To Sabrina H,
aka Samantha Danger Sparkle,
for all your support and encouragement.

Prologue

Chicago, Illinois, October 1964

Allison Stiles gathered up a book by her favorite romance author in one hand and a cup of tea in the other, then crossed the padded alphabet flooring and stepped out onto the enclosed front porch of her Rogers Park home. The neighborhood was old but well kept, the people warm and inviting. The shouts of children playing in the street drew her attention for a brief moment.

She wrapped a thin shawl around her shoulders and settled comfortably into the double-wide porch swing, set her teacup on the nearby window ledge, and opened her book to the first page. Given the week she'd had, she welcomed this chance to unwind, to do nothing but kick back and relax.

"I don't know what we're going to do with these two. They're headed for juvenile hall, I tell you that."

Principal Garner's harsh rebuke swirled around inside her head like the colors from a child's kaleidoscope, forcing her to set aside the book in favor of a sip of calming, herbal tea. As much as she hated to admit it, the man was right. Benny and Phillip were a handful and quickly getting on the edge of her very last nerve.

"We're sorry, Sis." Benny's apology filled her

thoughts.

"We didn't mean to do anything bad. Honest." Phillip's younger, softer voice tugged on her heartstrings.

Her brothers' penchant for trouble and the subsequent call to the principal's office was just the icing on the cake. She'd spent the entire week wiping runny noses and disinfecting child after child in an effort to keep this first round of seasonal flu from infecting her and everyone around her. She needed more than a cup of tea and a great read. She desperately needed a vacation. Unfortunately, her obligations didn't allow much down time.

At the very least she needed a distraction of some sort.

The loud slam of a car door and a man's muttered curse pulled her from this latest bout of self-pity and to the closest window. With the tips of her fingers, she slid the hand-made paper skeleton aside and stared out across her toy-strewn yard.

There in front of her, his arms filled with boxes, minus the one he'd dropped on the ground, stood the most handsome man she'd ever seen. A real-life Adonis, complete with dark, wavy hair and broad shoulders. When he turned toward the porch, she was gifted with an unencumbered view of his narrow hips and taut backside, both of which were encased in a pair of impossibly tight jeans.

She swallowed back the lump in her throat and licked her suddenly-dry lips.

As distractions go…this one was darned-near perfect.

Chapter One

So this was Rogers Park.

Eric Thomas shut the trunk of his '62 Buick and arched his back, working out the kinks earned from lifting heavy boxes for the past three hours. The October sun shone brightly, and he raised a hand to shade his eyes, turning full circle to assess both his new neighborhood and the brick bungalow he'd now be calling home.

The house, inherited from a maternal uncle, wasn't exactly the type of place he imagined himself living in when he moved back to Chicago. His plan had been to move into one of the fancy new high-rise buildings along Michigan Avenue or Lakeshore Drive. He'd pictured filling the spacious apartment with nice furniture, especially his brand new twenty-one inch, color television and hi-fi console.

Fate, it would seem, had other plans.

He'd spent a good portion…okay, maybe all…of his savings investing in a new business venture. He and his best friend Brad had decided to open their own ad agency. A place where their forward-thinking wouldn't be shut down by some stuffy old men who'd not changed their way of doing things in twenty-odd years.

On the plus side, at least the older home would give him the room he needed to get the business going. Until Brad arrived and they settled on a permanent location for their agency, he could easily run the first stages of their plans from the comfort of a home office. That is, as soon as someone from Illinois Bell arrived to convert the current party line to a private one. As friendly a neighborhood as Roger Park was supposed to be, he intended to keep his business and personal life private. Something virtually impossible while sharing a telephone line.

"Hey there, you must be the Thomas kid."

He turned. An older man stood on the cement stoop of the house to the right of his. "Yes, I am," he said. "Eric Thomas. You must be either Mr. Dunston or Mr. Collier."

The man choked out a smoker's cough followed by a rough chuckle. "I'm Collier. Teddy Dunston's on your other side. He and his missus are away for a few days visiting their grandchildren."

"It's nice to make your acquaintance, Mr. Collier—"

Collier shook his head. "Call me Jack. Nobody, other than the Stiles boys call me mister." He nodded toward the house directly across the street.

A large, fenced-in yard, filled from one edge to the other with toys set off alarms in Eric's head. Kids. They had kids. And, by the looks of it, quite a few.

He didn't do children very well, not that he'd ever had much reason to. He turned back to Jack Collier and asked, "Are there a lot of kids in the neighborhood?"

"Not as many as there used to be. If it weren't for Allison and her pile of noisy rascals, you might mistake this end of the block for a cemetery. And, heaven knows, most of us will be there sooner than we'd like."

Grinning at the man's comment, Eric nodded his

head in agreement and lifted the brown box at his feet. "It was nice meeting you."

"You too." Waving his hand as he made his way across his porch, Jack Collier added, "If you need anything, feel free to ask."

"Thanks. I'll keep that in mind."

He'd made it up onto the porch, brown box in tow, when a loud jolt of music rent the air. A whimsical lyric about dancing monsters, graveyards, and the upcoming holiday, the song was currently topping the charts.

Halloween. Kids. Noise.

He made himself a mental note: avoid 'Old Mother Hubbard' and her brood at all costs.

****

Eric awoke with jolt. The sound of a crying child permeated his foggy, sleep-deprived brain. He sat up in the bed and struggled to acclimate himself to his surroundings.

Tuesday. It was Tuesday, wasn't it? Chicago, right? He pinched the bridge of his nose with his thumb and forefinger to ward off an impending headache.

Perhaps you shouldn't have had that final drink last night. Or, the four before it.

At thirty-one, he was definitely getting too old to spend an evening schmoozing a potential client with expensive scotch. Not only would his wallet pay the price, but also his body and aching head.

The cry came again, louder this time. He swung his feet to the floor and reached for the alarm clock. Six-forty-two. *What the devil?*

Shuffling to the window, he fisted the blackout curtains and pushed them aside.

A man, most-likely 'Mr. Hubbard', was wrestling

his screaming toddler into the house across the street. Once the door shut behind them, a semblance of order was restored.

Short-lived it would appear when the door opened again and a woman descended the four steps into the yard. She had a sign of some sort under one arm and wielded a sledge hammer in her opposite hand.

As badly as his head hurt, and as much as he craved the dark solitude of his bedroom, an outright laugh escaped him.

The woman, five-foot-two at the most, probably weighed less than the tool she carried. He gave her the once-over. Despite her diminutive height, her body was one luscious curve after another. He blinked and let go of the curtain's edge, only to lift it a second time.

Long blonde hair cascaded across her slim shoulders, landing just above her narrow waist. Her hips flared out nicely, a shapely counter balance to her perfectly-rounded breasts.

His body stirred unexpectedly, but he dismissed the reaction as a regular early-morning occurrence. He let the curtain drop again. For all of five seconds.

Cursing his weakness for nicely built women, he pushed the heavy material aside for the third time. While he'd been doing his semi-best to ignore her, she'd made her way to the middle of the massive yard. Placing the pointed end of the wooden stake on the ground, she raised the hammer in the air and dropped the heavy steel head down firmly against the top of the stake. She repeated the hammering process another two times until the sign stood by itself.

Bewitched Day Care:
A Magical Place for Your Child

Cute slogan. The creative adman side of his brain acknowledged the catchy phrasing. Yet, all the practical side could see were the two words...day and care. Visions of screaming kids filled his thoughts, aggravating an already pounding head.

Mental note number two: move to the back bedroom, away from the street.

****

Allison gathered an armful of toys and tiptoed across the playroom. Eight tiny little bodies were stretched out on cots, eyes closed and blessedly quiet for their scheduled nap time.

After depositing the toys in their proper spaces, she took a seat in the far corner of the room and reached for a bracing cup of coffee. The opening theme to her favorite daytime soap, *Another World*, played softly on the ten-inch black and white in the corner.

"Whew," she whispered. "I thought Jasper was never going to go down."

Her assistant and best friend, Willa Abbott, chuckled and passed her a cookie. "Perhaps your heart wasn't in the storytelling and he sensed it."

Allison did her best to feign surprise. "Excuse me?"

Willa raised her finger, wagging it back in forth in front of Allison's face. "Don't play innocent with me. I saw you glancing out the window. Repeatedly. And each time you did, you lost your place in the story."

"I was distracted." Pausing, she added, "By the blowing leaves."

"Yeah, right. I know exactly what...or should I say who...you were looking at."

"I don't have the foggiest—"

"Stow it. I've been watching Mr. Tall and Hunky too. When I wasn't watching these little darlings, that is."

Allison chuckled. She could never put anything over on her childhood friend. The two of them could read one another like a couple of well-worn books. "He is rather dreamy, isn't he?"

"Compared to this neighborhood of retirees and middle-aged, married men, he's the top of the heap." A soft sigh proceeded Willa's whispered, "He's as handsome as Napoleon Solo and even sexier than Dr. Kildare."

As discreetly as possible, Allison raised the edge of Billy Parson's handmade pumpkin and peered out the playroom window. The object of her recent fantasies was outside raking his lawn. Dressed in a U of M sweatshirt and pair of rather snug-fitting jeans, her new neighbor was more than just top of the heap. He *was* the heap and then some.

Not nearly as cautious about being seen, Willa lifted the decoration away from the window and nodded toward the street. "So, are you going to go over and introduce yourself?"

"I thought about it," she admitted. "You know...welcome him to the neighborhood and all."

"You could take him a batch of your famous choco-blast cookies."

"Yes." The idea, she realized, had definite merit. "I guess I could do that given I want to be a good neighbor."

Willa let out a snort of a laugh and then quickly covered her mouth. Fortunately, her less-than-ladylike outburst hadn't disturbed the sleeping children. "A good neighbor…right. If I wasn't already dating someone, I'd be over there myself in a heartbeat. With cookies and any other treat I could think of to offer."

Allison shot her glare. "You're incorrigible."

"Yeah, I know. But I'm not the one who hasn't had a date in over two years."

Chapter Two

Eric shifted from one foot to the other, balancing the box of office supplies he'd purchased on his hip while lifting the grocery bag from the trunk with his opposite hand.

He'd spent the morning touring office space in mid-town Chicago and still not found anything within their price range. It looked as if the Thomas-Watson Agency would have to flourish a bit longer in its makeshift digs.

Thank heaven courting clients could be done in a restaurant, or the client's office, rather than in the cramped confines of his back room.

A noise drew his attention from his office-hunting dilemma and toward the daycare across the street. The petite blonde was leading a line of small children through a maze of toys.

Her long hair blew across her cheeks with each gust of wind, and she reached up to brush the errant strands off her face. His body tightened when he imagined her fingertips stroking his cheek in the same way.

He shook his head, dislodging the thought. The last thing he needed was the complication of a woman. Especially one who came saddled with a bunch of noisy kids.

Yeah, but they do eventually go home, you know.

Rather than acknowledge his inner voice of reason, he shifted his gaze and scanned the rest of the daycare's large yard. Another woman, taller, thinner, with jet black hair was organizing a game of tag among a few of the older children.

And despite the noisy diversion of their laughter, his attention was drawn back to the blonde. All around her, activity had stopped. Three little girls sat in silence at her feet.

She'd taken a seat on the front steps and lifted one of the smallest of the bunch onto her lap. Even surrounded by a handful of children, her tapered slacks and t-shirt covered in bright splashes of primary colors, she exuded an allure that set his nerves on edge.

She bent to listen to something the child was saying, and he found himself straining to hear as well. The faint sound of the child's cries drew her obvious compassion, and she gathered the little boy to her chest.

Lucky kid.

He stomped up the porch stairs, cursing the fact he could be so easily distracted. Mental note number three: stop ogling your sexy neighbor.

****

Later that evening, Eric poured himself another cup of coffee. One of the benefits, albeit a very unhealthy one, was the constant access to caffeine he got working less than a hundred feet from his kitchen. He pushed stacks of papers from one side of the desk to the other. He'd been struggling all day on a presentation for a local bakery chain that specialized in what they called all-natural ingredients. Usually anything to do with food and he was flush with ideas. Yet, for some reason, he couldn't wrap his head around this new health food kick. Organic, the woman had called it.

Dunking the sample cookie in his coffee, he took a bite. A shudder worked its way from head to toe. Give him a *Twinkie* or a cream filled cupcake and he could create the campaign blindfolded. How was he supposed to come up with a slogan for something that tasted like cardboard with unrefined sugar sprinkled very sparsely on top?

A knock pulled him from yet another unproductive stab at a slogan and to his front door. He wasn't expecting anyone. Yet, as he'd found out over the past week, his elderly neighbors loved stopping by to shoot the bull. He yanked open the door, fully expecting to see either Jack Collier or Teddy Dunston standing on the porch.

Instead, the kiddie-goddess stood on his threshold, a plate of baked goods balanced on her outstretched hands.

"Hello," he said.

She took a small bite of her lower lip and then swept her tongue across the indentation. His heart hammered against his chest with a frighteningly uneven rhythm. His mouth literally watered at the thought of brushing his own tongue along the seam of her perfectly-kissable lips.

"Hi, I'm Allison Stiles, from across the street." She glanced back over her shoulder in the direction of the daycare and then turned her gaze back to his. "I brought you a welcome-to-the-neighborhood gift."

She had the most remarkable light green eyes that sparkled when she talked. A dusting of freckles crossed the very bridge of her nose and feathered out onto her cheeks. Her breasts, often on prominent display in his most recent dreams, pushed enticingly against her soft, angora sweater. Tempting, but in a rather innocent way.

He swallowed, silently cursing the sudden dryness in his throat. "Thank you. I'm Eric. Eric Thomas." He tightened his grip on the brass door handle and tugged until the door was fully open. "I've just made a fresh pot of coffee if you'd like to come in for a cup."

She hesitated and his gut clenched. Had his invitation been too forward? Was she about to bolt and run?

"I suppose I could stay for a few minutes. My brothers are at basketball practice until six-thirty."

Stepping back, he extended his arm and motioned her into the entranceway. "So, what's on the plate?"

"Just some banana muffins and choco-blast cookies."

"Choco-blast cookies?" The name matched her perfectly...upbeat...exciting.

"It's my own recipe. Lots of chocolate, some chopped pecans, and then some more chocolate."

He took the plate from her hands and led the way to the kitchen, sidestepping a half-dozen unpacked boxes in their path. "Sounds...uh...chocolatey." When she fell into step behind him, he warned, "Watch your step, it's chaos in here."

She giggled, the sound totally at odds with her womanly curves.

"Don't worry about. Moving is hard work. As for the cookies, I guess the name is a bit over the top. Hopefully you like chocolate"

Once she'd taken a seat at the round, wooden table, he poured her a cup of the promised coffee. "Actually, I love chocolate. I'm not so sure about the calories though. I haven't joined a gym since moving back to Chicago. I should probably go easy on the cookies."

She gathered the cup in her hands. "Moved back from where?"

"Detroit. At least for the past six years."

"Do you have family there?" she asked.

He wondered if she was fishing for his marital status, or just making small talk. "No family. I was working for a large ad agency." He set the cream and sugar on the table in front of her, before adding, "My parents actually live not far from here. They own a dairy farm a few miles outside Moline."

Allison splashed a small amount of cream in her cup. "I met your mother once. She came to visit your uncle after he became ill."

"I have to admit, I didn't know my uncle that well. I hadn't seen him since I went off to U of M. Even on my few trips home, I never made an effort to visit." He took a sip of his own coffee. "It was quite a surprise to find out he'd left me this house."

A shrug lifted her slim shoulders and drew his attention back to her peachy complexion. And those freckles.

"Perhaps it was his way of getting you to come home."

"I guess." He reached for one of the chocolate-laden cookies and took a bite. The flavor exploded in his mouth...a decadent temptation equaled only by the beautiful woman seated across from him.

"Too much chocolate?" Her gaze met his, her green eyes wide with question.

He licked a crumb from his lip and pulled it into his mouth. "Wow." He held what little was left of the cookie up for inspection. "This has got to be the best cookie I've ever had."

Her smile widened. "Good. I brought you a half-dozen of them, but you might want to pace yourself. They're very rich and can easily become addictive."

"I should say so. They're already working their magic on me." He crammed the last piece of cookie in his mouth and let the chocolate melt on his tongue. "You should own a bakery."

"Other than cookies and the occasional muffin, I'm not much of a cook."

Somehow he doubted that. After all, she already had him hot and bothered.

"I've been working on an ad campaign all afternoon and can't get a handle on how to present the product. After eating one of your cookies, I can imagine an entire layout."

"You can?" The slight squeak in her voice ratcheted up his pulse rate at least ten points.

"Yes. Decadent, Delicious and Devilishly Delightful. Your mascot would be a playful little devil with a chocolate pitchfork."

She swallowed the last of her coffee and then stood to leave. "I'd better get back home. Benny and Phillip will be descending on my kitchen in a few minutes. I'd rather they eat their supper first…before they attack the cookies."

He walked her to the door, reluctant to see her leave. "Probably a good idea."

When she stepped onto the porch, he found himself struggling for something else to say, to prolong her short visit. Anything, he realized, to keep Allison Stiles within reach.

Unfortunately, nothing came immediately to mind.

Chapter Three

"So, dish." Willa leaned across the width of the arts-and-crafts table and lowered her voice. "What's he like? Did he absolutely declare his undying love the moment he tasted your cookies?"

Allison pushed back an outright laugh. Willa had been playing twenty-questions for the past half hour. In hindsight, she probably shouldn't have told her friend about visiting the new neighbor.

"The cookies are yummy but not magical."

"Oh, please. I took some home with me one time, and my goofy brothers were tripping over themselves on their way out the door to propose marriage."

"Your brothers are fourteen and sixteen."

"Doesn't matter. I'm telling you, those cookies are an aphrodisiac."

"Don't be ridiculous. Cookies are just cookies, nothing more. Chocolate makes you happy." Leaning closer to where Willa sat, she whispered, "Not horny."

Willa chuckled and then smothered the sound with her fingertips. "There's nothing wrong with a bit of both."

If there was one thing Allison loved about her best friend it was her unabashed honesty…as crude as it sometimes was. Willa loved life and loved men…not necessarily in that same order. Her latest boyfriend, Scott was, no doubt a lucky, lucky man.

The children were nearly finished with their lunches and would soon be eager for a half-hour or so outside. Allison pushed herself away from the craft table and went to check on her six little charges. "Has everyone finished eating?"

"Everyone but Tommy," Sally said. "He only has crackers and butter. And no milk."

It was a known fact the Boyd family had run into dire straits lately with Mr. Boyd's sudden illness and additional medical bills. She hadn't realized it was so bad they couldn't provide a proper lunch for their youngest son. Allison silently cursed herself for being so wrapped up in her flighty discussion with Willa that she'd not paid more attention to the lunch table.

While admiring her handsome new neighbor had certainly been the diversion she'd wished for, shirking her responsibilities toward the children was unthinkable. Irresponsible. And if there was one thing she understood better than most, it was responsibility.

She waved her arm to encompass the children seated around the two square tables. "You can all meet Miss Willa by the door. She'll help you with your coats. Tommy," she said, turning to the four year old, "You sit here for another minute or two."

She went to the small refrigerator at the back of the room and withdrew a plastic tub of what Willa called 'spares'. Intended for children who had forgotten their lunch, the tub contained fruit, jelly, and celery sticks. She also took out a bottle of fresh milk. From the overhead cupboard, she withdrew peanut butter, a tin of potted meat, and a loaf of brown bread.

Everything balanced in her arms, she took a seat at Tommy's side. "I can make you a sandwich of either

PB&J or potted meat while you nibble on some celery."

The little boy raised his head and met her gaze, his saucer-like brown eyes filled with tears. "Momma was gonna make me egg sandwiches before she left for her work, but I told her to give the eggs to my daddy 'cause he's sick."

Her heart clenched, and she blinked back her own tears. "That's very generous of you, Tommy, but you're a growing boy and need food too."

"I told her to make me crackers and butter." He scrunched up his tiny nose. "But I really don't like them much."

She offered the child a smile, and asked, "So, which is it? Potted meat or peanut butter and jelly."

"Is it strawberry jelly?"

"Yes."

He smiled broadly, his gap-toothed grin tugging on her heartstrings. Pushing the jar of peanut butter in her direction, he told her, "Good, 'cause I love strawberry jelly."

Allison started to work on the sandwich. "You've got to promise me you'll always let me know if you've not got a proper lunch."

Tommy swallowed his mouthful of celery and nodded. "I promise Miss Ally."

Later that day, she and Willa packed up a small basket of baked goods, canned tuna, an extra loaf of bread, and a jar of Tommy's favored jelly and set it by the door. Mrs. Boyd was always the last to arrive so giving her the gifted items wouldn't…shouldn't…cause any undue embarrassment for either of them.

It wasn't much but, hopefully, the few food stuffs would get them to Mrs. Boyd's next payday.

****

It had been a few days since she'd seen Eric, other than the one evening he'd left his house about six. He'd been dressed in a pair of casual slacks and sports coat. His dark hair had fallen rather rakishly across his forehead, and he'd run his long fingers through the curls to push them back in place.

Her pulse had raced at the sight of him. At the thought of how those same long fingers would feel running through her hair. Or perhaps, the racing was caused by the clandestine way she was spying on him from behind the dotted Swiss curtains on her bedroom window.

"Penny for your thoughts."

Allison started at the sound of Willa's voice. "They're not worth a penny." She motioned toward the corner of the playroom where the children were working diligently at their easels. Finger paint sloshed from the plastic cups and onto the well-worn tarp beneath their feet. "I was thinking about how badly I need to purchase a new tarp."

"Yeah, and you were thinking that while staring out the window at Mr. Tall, Dark, and Gorgeous' porch." Willa nudged her arm playfully. "Maybe if you stare long enough he'll actually come outside."

She was working up a witty reply when the phone rang, pulling her from her thoughts and back to reality. Allison grabbed for the wall-mounted handset and pressed it to her ear. "Bewitched Day Care, this is Allison."

"Miss Stiles, this is Principal Garner."

"Hello, Principal Garner. What can I do for you?"

"I'm afraid we have a situation with your brother

Benny, and I need you to come to the school immediately."

"But, I can't—" Allison looked up from her study of the telephone cord to see Willa waving her hand, shooing her out the door. "Okay, sir, I'll be there as soon as possible."

The moment Allison replaced the handset, Willa asked, "Which one this time, and what has he done?"

It was then that she realized she'd not even asked. Calls from the principal's office were becoming so frequent it no longer mattered what one of them had done, only that she handle it as quickly as possible.

"It's Benny, but I didn't stay on the line long enough to find out what he's done." She glanced around the room, happy to see the children still engrossed in their artwork. "I can't leave you with six...it's too much for one person."

Willa placed her hands firmly on her hips. "I can manage. You go do what you need to do."

"How about I run across the street and ask Mrs. Dunston to come help. She's great with her grandchildren."

"If it'll put your mind at ease," Willa agreed. "I don't want you worrying about me when you've got bigger issues with your brother."

Allison threw on her lightweight jacket and dashed across the street. The Dunston's car wasn't in the driveway, but she kept her fingers crossed that Sophie Dunston was home anyway. Her hands shaking with impatience, she leaned on the doorbell.

Darn her brother and his recent penchant for trouble. Didn't he realize how inconvenient his misbehavior was for everyone concerned? She pressed the bell a second time.

Crap and double crap. She spared a quick glance toward the day care. She had no doubt Willa could handle things. That said, she also hated putting such a responsibility on the one person she counted on most. Drawing a deep breath for courage, she bounded down the Dunstan's steps and onto Eric Thomas' porch.

Fortunately, he answered on the first push of the bell.

"Eric, I'm so sorry to bother you, but I'm in a bind."

He pulled the door open. "Come in and tell me how I can help."

"I don't have time to explain much, other than to say I have to go to the school and bail my brother out of another jam. Yet, I can't leave Willa alone at the daycare with six children. Some days it's a madhouse with two of us and way too much for one person."

"Uh…you want me to help out with the kids?"

"Yes, if you wouldn't mind." Seeing his hesitation, she tried to think of something reassuring to say. "It'll only be an hour tops. I promise."

He shrugged and grabbed his jacket from the peg by the door. "I don't know much about kids. As a matter of fact, I don't know anything about kids except they're noisy and dirty."

"My little angels will be very good. I promise."

He shot her a look of disbelief. The panic she could see in his expression only highlighted his dark eyes and perfect features.

"I won't have to change diapers, will I?"

"No, of course not. We've only got two in training pants, and Willa will do the honors if necessary." They parted ways at her driveway. She sat in her car and waited while Eric climbed the stairs leading up to the front door. Once he'd opened the door and gone inside, she pulled her car into reverse and backed out onto the street.

Please let them all behave. And please help me to not kill my brother. Hopefully this afternoon wouldn't prove to be the end of her short-lived friendship with her handsome neighbor.

****

"Hi, I'm Eric." He held out his hand to Allison's assistant. "I've been dragooned as your backup."

He could see she was biting back on an outright fit of laughter and the thought scared him just a bit. Or maybe more than a bit.

She grasped his hand in hers and then pulled back quickly. "I'm Willa. Here, let me get you a damp rag."

He looked down at his hand. Bright red coated his palm. He took the cloth she offered and began swiping at the paint. "Arts and crafts, I see."

She winced. "Sorry. I forgot I'd just cleaned some brushes."

"No problem, Willa." He slid out of his jacket and set it on the chair farthest from the children. "What can I do to help?"

"Perhaps you could assist Bobby and Carole. They're working on their pumpkins."

Eric weaved his way between the tables, easels and boxes of craft supplies, careful not to bump into anything. When Allison had shown up at his door and asked for his help, he'd thought of refusing, of coming up with some lame excuse in order to avoid the day care.

23

But then she'd raised her head and he'd seen the tears glistening in her eyes, held staunchly at bay by no more than sheer determination, and he'd been unable to say 'no'. After all, it was only an hour. And despite his gross lack of knowledge and experience where children were concerned, what possible harm could he do?

Chapter Four

Allison slid from behind the driver's seat and motioned both brothers up the front stairs. "You two are grounded for a week, including television. Which means, no *Addam's Family* or *McHale's Navy*."

"That's not fair. I didn't do anything," Phillip argued.

"Don't give me that. If you hadn't been taunting a sixth grader in the first place, Benny wouldn't have felt the need to come to your defense." She rounded the car and caught hold of the brothers' shirt sleeves, tugging just hard enough to get their attention. "If you two behave, you might be out of the dog house before Halloween. Maybe."

The boys turned right at the front door and headed up to their rooms. Letting go of a long, cleansing sigh, Allison turned left, intending to thank Eric for his help and relieve him of his duties.

She stepped into the main playroom and came to an immediate halt. There, in the middle of the craft area, hunkered down on a child-sized chair, sat Eric. His light brown slacks and caramel colored shirt were covered from top to bottom with a rainbow of haphazard designs. Bright orange paint stained his leather loafers. White craft glue dripped from the hem of his shirt. Across his chest was a wet patch of...

Oh, god...someone had thrown up. The familiar

stench hung in the air.

She stepped around a pile of blocks and rushed across the room. "What happened?" He didn't respond other than to glare at her as if she had three heads.

Willa came to their side, a wet washcloth clutched in her fist. "Here, Eric." Handing him the cloth, she explained, "Bobby was eating crayons again."

Eric dashed at the front of his shirt with the damp cloth and then pushed himself to his feet. "Good, you're back. I've got to go." Without waiting for her apology, he ran for the door.

She thought of following him but, instead, turned back to a tearful Bobby and lifted the boy into her arms. "Crayons? I thought we talked about not eating the art supplies."

****

Allison shifted nervously on Eric's porch, her finger poised above the doorbell. His jacket lay limp over her arm, a testament to his quick escape earlier that day. Drawing a breath, she pushed the ringer and waited.

And waited.

She was about to turn and walk away when the door sprung open, in much the same fashion as the way her jaw dropped to her knees.

Eric stood on the threshold wearing little more than his usual snug fitting jeans. His bare chest taunted her, begging to be touched. Stroked. The finger paint he'd sported earlier had been replaced by house paint, its pungent odor assailing her senses, while its subdued shade splashed its way across his midriff, narrow denim-clad hips, and down his long legs.

Tentatively, she held out her arm. "I've come to

return your jacket. You left it…"

He pulled the door open all the way and stepped back. "Come in. I'm just finishing up the first coat of paint on the back bedroom."

"The front bedroom gets better light." She silently cursed the stupid comment and followed him into the living room.

He turned slowly. His brow arched and lips twitched as if he were fighting back a laugh. "I realize that. Unfortunately, it's not as quiet as the back of the house."

Embarrassment flooded her cheeks with warmth. "Oh, right." Again, she offered him the jacket, but he shook his head.

"Can you just lay it over there? My hands are sticky." He held them out for her inspection.

"I'm really, really sorry about today." Her apology came out on a rush. "I'd like to pay to have your slacks and shirt dry cleaned."

Another smile tugged at his firm lips. "It's not necessary. Both the shirt and khakis were machine washable."

"What about your shoes? They looked expensive."

He held up his hand. "Don't worry about it. I'll drop them off at the shoemaker. He should have some solvent that will take out the paint but not harm the leather."

She back-pedaled toward the door, hesitant to leave yet uncertain as to whether or not he wanted her to stay. "I should be getting back. The boys are doing their homework, and—"

"Would you like to stay for a drink?" He drew a long breath. His shoulders rose and fell, drawing her gaze back to his chest. "Or if you don't drink, I could make coffee. Or tea."

"I wouldn't mind a glass of wine if you have it."

The smile teasing his lips earlier came out in full force. "Red or white?"

"Red, please."

Eric motioned toward the couch. "Have a seat. I'll just grab a shirt, a couple of glasses, and the bottle."

Forget the shirt. Her naughty little conscience protested the very thought of him covering up such a nicely sculpted chest. Yet the lady in her remained silent.

He returned moments later, the promised bottle of wine in one hand, two glasses in the other and wearing a dark blue t-shirt emblazoned with the words: *Beatles, North American Tour, 1964.*

"You saw The Beatles?" she asked, her gaze pulled toward the colorful artwork on a darker background.

He set the wine and glasses on the coffee table and then tugged on the hem of the shirt so the writing at the bottom of the design was apparent. "Yes, here in Chicago just last month."

"Was it as great as the newspapers made it out to be?"

"I guess so," he said with a shrug. "It was hard to actually hear the music because of the screaming girls. However, my new client had tickets and didn't want to be the only adult among a throng of excited teenagers, including his own two daughters, so I went with him."

After taking a seat beside her on the couch, Eric poured the wine and then passed her a glass.

"Willa listens to all the new English groups." She took a sip of her wine and continued. "Personally, I'm still a big Elvis fan."

He raised his own glass in a mock salute. "Me too. Nobody can top *The King*."

She shot him a grin. "I feel silly admitting it, but I've actually seen *Viva Las Vegas* three times in the theater."

"Not so silly," he assured her. "The title song is one of my favorites. It's got a real upbeat feel about it."

They finished their wine, and he poured them both a second glass. She knew she should have refused, but just the thought of relaxing, letting her guard down even for a few minutes was a luxury she rarely enjoyed. Not wanting the peace of the moment to end, she scrambled for a topic of conversation.

"How's your hunt for office space coming along?"

"Not nearly as good as I'd hoped. Brad's scheduled to arrive on Monday, the second, and I wanted to have at least a couple of options to show him."

"He's your best friend?"

"Yep, since college. Even after he and Stacy married, we managed a racquet ball game at least once a week."

She shifted on the comfy couch and took another sip of wine. "A best friend is good. I'd be lost without Willa."

"You two make a good pair. It's obvious you both adore those kids." A faint smile bent the corners of his full lips. "Can I ask…are you…uh…seeing someone?"

She plucked at the hem of her sweater, one of her more aggravating habits. Shaking her head for emphasis, she admitted, "Between my business and my repeated trips to the school because of my brothers, I'm lucky if I have time to eat. Dating would be an all-out fantasy."

Was it her imagination, or had he closed the distance between them? Had his leg always been so close she could readily imagine their thighs brushing?

"You know what they say...all work and no play."

She gulped the next drink of her wine in an effort to chase away a suddenly dry throat. "What do you mean? I play every day. Well, maybe just Monday through Friday. And with toddlers, but still..."

His hearty laugh set her racing heartbeat into overdrive. "I was thinking more along the lines of something not involving crayons."

The gentle pressure of his fingertips against her chin forced her head up until their gazes locked. "You were?" She bit her lip, embarrassed by the squeak in her voice.

He leaned closer and pressed his lips to hers. Turning his head slowly from side-to-side, he dusted her mouth with his. "Yes, I was," he whispered, his lips barely leaving hers as he spoke.

A nervous giggle slipped out. "No crayons is probably the way to go. Definitely."

Eric pulled her into his arms and lowered his head for another kiss. She went willingly...captive of both his strong embrace and the heady taste of wine on his lips.

The kiss was perfect. Or at least what she imagined to be perfection. It had been ages since she'd had something for comparison, but she felt certain it had never been this good.

His sigh fluttered across her face and he raised his head. "Wow. I've been wanting to do that since the first time I saw you."

The infuriating squeak was back in her voice. "You have?"

"And quite honestly, I thought you were married with a bunch of kids at the time. Yet, I still had this feeling."

"What feeling?"

He brushed his thumb across her lower lip. "Like not kissing you was going to be impossible." As if to prove his point, he lowered his head and pressed his lips to hers. When he nipped at her lower lip, she gasped and he teased her with his taste, yet waited for permission before deepening the kiss.

Allison parted her lips, granting him the access he'd requested.

Thud! Was that her heart beating so hard she feared it might jump out of her chest?

Her head spun like one of the colorful tops in the playroom of her daycare. His finesse, mixed with a glass and a half of wine, was doing a real number on her equilibrium. She needed to regain control of her senses. She had responsibilities. She had…

He made a second and third sweep of her mouth, coaxing her to return the kiss. He tasted of wine and mint. The silky feel of his mouth was enticing, intoxicating. She easily imagined herself locked in Eric's arms, a willing captive to everything he had to offer.

The weight of his hand resting lightly against her breast drew her back to reality with a jolt. This was escalating far faster than she was used to, than she wanted. She covered his hand with her own and pulled it away from her body.

"I'm sorry," he said softly. "I—"

"No, don't apologize. We both got caught up in the kiss."

Allison pushed herself to her feet. Her knees wobbled, and she braced herself with a hand to Eric's shoulder.

"Are you okay?"

She nodded. "Yes. I'm fine, and I really do need to get home. No doubt my brothers have gotten themselves into mischief while I was gone."

"I can walk you, if you'd like."

"No. I can't let you do that."

His eyes widened and the smile she loved so much turned down. "Why not?"

"Because it would make it even harder to say goodnight."

Chapter Five

Eric stood at the living room window, a cup of coffee in one hand, and the inside edge of the drapes in his other. He'd spent the past half hour trying to talk himself back to work. Yet, the sound of children's laughter, the sight of Allison leading a march around the perimeter of her large yard, had drawn him to the window more times than he cared to count.

It had been two days since he'd actually talked to her. He'd made a mistake the night they'd kissed. He'd rushed her. It had been obvious to him by the way she'd approached the deepened kiss, she was a novice at the steamier side of things.

Maybe even a virgin.

The thought had come to him within minutes after she'd left and still nagged him every time he looked at her. He liked her, really liked her. Yet, he wasn't sure he possessed the patience, or the skill, required to woo such an inexperienced woman. No matter how great her kisses tasted.

And then there was the issue of the kids.

He'd been livid when he'd returned from her house covered in paint, glue, and stink. While he'd peeled his way out of his clothes, he'd made mental note number four: get a vasectomy.

That thought had fled as quickly as it had come. He did want a family eventually, but he wanted it one kid at a time, not a half dozen of them already fully formed. Not to mention her two brothers. From what he'd gathered, they were trouble with a capital T.

He let the drapes fall back into place. With a presentation due day after tomorrow, work took priority over everything else. Even the beautiful blonde who'd turned him on full tilt with only a few, albeit great, kisses.

Nothing short of an emergency was going to take him away from his story boards.

****

Allison leaned on her garden rake and spared a quick glance toward Eric's porch. It had been two days since they'd kissed. Had she scared him away for good? No doubt he had little time to spare for someone who panicked so easily.

Silly girl. He obviously prefers his women more experienced. Less encumbered by responsibility.

She shot her cruel inner voice a mental glare before turning her attention back to the children playing in the yard. The wind had blown all night long, and their usual play area was buried in leaves from the half dozen trees in her yard. It didn't seem to matter one bit to her charges as they ran from one side to the other, dragging their feet through the crisp leaves she'd managed to rake into some semblance of order.

"You look as if you could use some help."

The sound of Eric's deep voice drew her attention from the dirt to where he stood at her gate. "Excuse me," she said, faltering for anything remotely coherent.

"The leaves. They seem to have taken over your yard."

She gave the rake a swish. "It does seem rather

foolish to try and rake them until after the children leave for the day."

He lifted the latch and stepped through the gate, making sure to secure the bolt after him. "I could help, if you'd like."

"Shouldn't you be at home working on some great ad campaign?" Even as she asked, she was sliding the rake in his direction. If manual labor kept him close, she was not beneath using it to her advantage.

Eric took the tool from her hand, his fingers brushing hers and lingering. Using his thumb, he stroked the back of her wrist. "I'm stalled. I thought perhaps some fresh air might clear the creative fog."

"Mr. Eric," a tiny voice called out, drawing his gaze to the little girl at their feet, pulling his hand from Allison's.

"Hello, Carole. Nice to see you again."

She grinned, her tongue peeking through the spot where two front teeth should have been. "Bobby's not here today, so no throwing up on you."

His chuckle was loud, drawing Carole's giggle, and Allison's corresponding smile. "That's good to know."

Once Carole had run off to rejoin her friends, Eric began on the leaves. Allison reached for a second rake and fell into step at his side.

"What made you want to run a daycare center?" he asked.

"Actually, it was my mother's pride and joy before she passed away. I guess you could say, I inherited the family business."

"I'm sorry, I didn't realize."

She shook her head, hoping to still his concern. "It's been a little over four years now."

"What about your father?"

"Pops passed away three years before her. Mom started the business right after he died. I was in my sophomore year at college, and my brothers were barely in grade school at the time. It was her way of earning a decent living and still taking care of us at the same time. When Mom passed, I took over the daycare and guardianship of the boys so it seemed natural to continue on with her plan."

"No other brothers or sisters?"

"We have an older brother, David. He was living in Indiana with his wife and twin girls at the time. His job kept him traveling a lot, so it wasn't feasible for him to take the boys too." She took a stab at a particularly stubborn bunch of leaves before adding, "David and his family live close now…in Batavia. Which is nice because he takes the boys off my hands every other weekend."

"Gives you break, does it?"

"Yes and a much needed one at that. I love my younger brothers dearly, but they can be a handful." His smile teased her, made her toes curl inside her sneakers.

"So I've heard. According to Jack Collier, your brothers keep everyone on their toes."

"That they do," she admitted.

Chimes rang from inside the house, the signal that outdoor time was ending. Eric glanced toward the slightly open window. "What was that?"

"Lunch bell," she said simply. "Playtime is over, at least for now."

"And later?"

"Lunch, followed by my favorite…quiet time."

"I have to admit, I'm in awe not only of your

devotion to these kids but also to your brothers. It's a lot for a young woman to take on alone."

"I'm not totally alone. I have Willa." She took the rake from his hand. "And possibly a new gardener."

He chuckled. "I'm much better at this than arts and crafts."

"Don't sell yourself short. Prior to his queasy stomach, Bobby created quite a lovely pumpkin under your tutelage."

"I do have some artistic background you know. It just doesn't usually revolve around finger paints, crayons, and glue."

"If you're game for more adventure, our Halloween party is Friday. There'll be punch, bobbing for apples, and treats."

"Choco-blast cookies perhaps?"

She laid her hand against his arm and smiled. "If you behave."

The quick shake of his head drew her stare like a magnet to the front of her fridge. "Behave? Now you're taking the fun out of it completely."

****

Eric couldn't believe how easily he'd acquiesced to Allison's party invitation. Add to that, his rather hasty decision to don a costume of his own, and he'd about decided he'd lost his marbles. He glanced at his mirrored reflection. If not his marbles, perhaps his sense of modesty. The blue tights clung to his legs like a second skin.

Thank heaven for the bright red cape. At least he could hide somewhat behind its yards and yards of material. The fellow at the costume shop had assured him *Superman* himself wouldn't be able to tell the difference. Given his audience would be made up of children not yet born when the original television series aired, he doubted they'd even notice he was wearing black high-top sneakers instead of red leather boots.

The moment he walked through the door of the day care, Eric was engulfed in a swarm of screaming children. Allison, he noticed, fought back an outright laugh while encouraging the children back to their chairs.

"Nice costume." Willa sidled up to his left and gave him a playful nudge. "Personally, I'd have gone for something a little less...uh...bright."

He shot her a sideways glance and chuckled. "This coming from someone dressed like a unicorn, complete with multi-colored, sparkling horn."

The party in full swing, he found he was actually enjoying himself. When they weren't throwing up on you, or crying, children weren't half-bad. He'd made an effort on a number of occasions to reach Allison, but she was always preoccupied with one child or another. Dressed as a colorful good witch, she'd certainly cast a spell on him.

His attention on Allison, it was a moment or two before he realized someone was tugging on his cape. He looked down into the smiling face of Bobby, the crayon muncher.

"Hi there, Champ." He squatted down to the small boy's level. "What can I do for you?"

"I just wanted to tell you I was sorry for being sick on you the other day." The threat of tears shone in the little fella's big brown eyes, and Eric had the urge to reach out and lift the boy into his arms.

Instead, he chose to brush his hand across the boy's

unruly blond curls. "That's okay. I know you couldn't help it. We all have bad days from time to time."

Bobby gave another tug on his cape. "Even Superman?"

"Yes, even Superman." He nodded toward the far side of the room. "Why don't we go bob for some of those juicy looking apples?"

Hand in hand, they walked across the room, the little boy's threat of tears replaced by a broad smile. A strange feeling tugged at Eric's heartstrings. When he looked up, he came face-to-face with Allison. And as if she could read his thoughts...his confusion...she smiled at him and gave him an understanding nod.

His heart clenched again, only this time he understood the rush of emotion. He was falling for Allison. Hard and fast.

By four-thirty all of the children had been picked up by their parents and gone off happily clutching their handmade decorations and treat bags filled with an assortment of fruit, cookies, and a few pieces of candy for good measure.

Willa and Allison were busy clearing the tables of leftover food and paper plates. "What can I do to help?" he asked.

Allison motioned toward the wild tangle of chairs. "If you wouldn't mind stacking the chairs in the corner, it would be a big help. No doubt this floor is going to require mopping."

No sooner had she spoken when he stepped in a glob of cupcake icing. Reaching for a napkin, he balanced on one foot and wiped the sole of his shoe. "No doubt indeed."

Her laughter drew his attention to her smile.

"You were a big hit with the children," she told him.

"Yeah," Willa chimed in. "I'm sure they couldn't wait to get home to tell their older brothers and sisters that they'd partied with Superman."

He bowed graciously and shot both women a broad grin. "What's a superhero for if not to show a bunch of kids how to bob for apples and make paper airplanes?" He paused briefly, and then added, "I had a great time today."

"Despite not having any experience with children?" Allison asked.

He shrugged and met her gaze. Her eyes twinkled with humor. "Hey, I'm just glad nobody got sick. This costume would have been a real pain to clean."

****

Allison sat cross-legged in the middle of the playroom floor. Eric had left a half hour earlier. Willa a few minutes afterward. She knew she should head upstairs and make supper for her brothers, yet she sat there replaying the events of the afternoon over and over in her head.

When Eric had shown up at the door in costume, her heart had soared with a mixture of feelings. The Superman outfit had certainly been a hit with the children, each one of them vying for time with their favorite comic book character.

The snug fit of the costume, although discreetly hidden beneath the cape, had drawn her attention over and over again. When he'd discarded the cape while they were cleaning up, her stomach had turned somersaults, and her pulse had run a marathon. And when Willa had caught her looking, she'd taken a teasing elbow to her side.

Despite her limited experience, she'd recognized her reaction for what it was...desire, pure and simple. With no serious physical relationship since college, perhaps it was time to bury her emotional baggage, and take another shot at romance. Assuming, of course, one would-be superhero was interested.

She pushed herself to her feet and headed off to make soup and sandwiches for herself and the boys. She'd promised them they could go down the block and play street hockey with their friends as long as they were home by dark.

They, in turn, had promised her they'd avoid any Devil's Night shenanigans.

Chapter Six

So much for empty promises.

Allison stood on her porch steps, armed with an oversize wastepaper basket, a long-handled broom, and her embarrassment. Not only had the boys gone against their promise of good behavior, but they'd done the unthinkable.

They TP'd Eric's porch and bushes.

Perhaps it wasn't them.

She pushed her inner-voice of hope aside. Of course it was her brothers. The chaotic mess had their names stamped all over it.

Blinking back tears of frustration, she glanced at her wristwatch and made her way across the street. Seven-thirty in the morning. With any luck, Eric was still asleep, and she could get the mess cleaned up before he realized what had happened.

She'd barely reached the bottom step of Eric's porch when the front door swung open. He stood there on the threshold in his usual uniform of tight jeans and dark t-shirt, his long fingers wrapped around a steaming mug of coffee.

"I see Devil's Night is no different here in Rogers Park than it was back in Michigan."

Tears welled up in her eyes, and she nodded. "I'll have this cleaned up before you know it."

"No, you won't." He stepped out onto the porch

and motioned her up the stairs. When she'd reached his side, he handed her the cup of coffee. "You'll stay here while I go and roust those brothers of yours and get them over here to do their own clean up."

The thought of protesting flashed through her mind, halted only by the look of determination in Eric's expression before he marched down the stairs, across the street, and through her gate.

Taking a seat on his porch stoop, she sipped at the coffee he'd given her and waited for him to return with her brothers in tow.

****

Eric strode up the stairs with purpose, intent on reading both boys the riot act. It wasn't so much the unsightly adornment of toilet paper he objected to, but rather Benny and Phillip's total disrespect for their sister. He had half a mind to turn both boys over his knee for a good, old-fashioned spanking.

Instead, he pounded loudly on their bedroom door before pushing it open and stepping inside.

Both boys sat up in their beds with a start.

"Good morning, fellows," Eric said, more cheerful than he felt at the moment.

"Uh…you're…uh Eric, right?" Benny asked.

"Yes, you know darn well who I am."

Phillip, the younger of the two, pushed himself to a fully seated position, his short legs dangling over the edge of the upper bunk. "What do you want? Where's Ally?"

"Your sister is sitting on my porch, drinking a cup of my best coffee, and waiting somewhat patiently for you two to get dressed and come clean up the mess you made in my yard."

"What are you talking about, man?" Benny grumbled. "What mess?"

Eric hunkered down on his heels beside the lower bunk until he was eye-to-eye with Benny. "You both know darned well 'what mess,' so don't play dumb with me. You might have your sister bending over backward for the two of you, but I've got no qualms with handing out some fitting punishment." He paused, letting his words sink in. "Perhaps missing tonight's trick or treating will have you thinking twice about playing pranks."

"You can't do that," Benny insisted. "You're not our father, our brother, or even a distant uncle."

"I might not be any of those," Eric agreed. "However, I am the man who's going to see you clean up your mess and apologize to your sister. That, or I'll be the fellow to call the cops and report your vandalism."

"You can't prove it was us," Phillip said, although his voice faltered, rather than held the conviction of an innocent.

"Your sister seems to believe it was you, so I'm inclined to side with her. Now, I'm going to wait out in the hall for three minutes. If you're not dressed and ready to walk across the street with me, I'm going to come back in here and drag you out in your pajamas for the entire neighborhood to see."

He was happy Allison hadn't moved from her seat on his stoop. He'd half expected her to start on the yards and yards of paper adornments. Yet, thankfully, she hadn't.

He gave both boys a nudge through Allison's front gate and across the street. "I'm glad to see you boys didn't test my patience."

A snort of displeasure filled the space between himself and Benny. "I'm only here because of my sister."

"Me too," Phillip added, the slight squeak in his voice just like his sister's and far more apologetic than defiant.

When they stood at the bottom of his porch steps, Benny glanced from Allison to Eric and back again before turning full-circle to take in the mess. "What makes you so sure it was us?"

Allison joined them at the bottom of the stairs and put her arm around Benny's shoulders, steering him toward the row of bushes. "For starters, when I caught you both sneaking up the stairs two hours after you'd already gone to bed, your story about forgetting to put away your bikes didn't hold true. Especially, given I'd seen them in the garage when I locked up for the night. Then, when I got up this morning and noticed this...uh...catastrophe, I put two and two together. Then, I checked and realized there were four packages of toilet paper missing from the daycare's inventory."

Eric handed the long-handled broom and a large, plastic garbage bag to Phillip, before turning back to meet Allison's warm smile. "I'll refresh your cup of coffee while these fellows get to work."

Allison returned to her seat on the stoop. "Thank you. I'll stay here and keep an eye on the boys."

It took Benny and Phillip over an hour to remove the thin tissue streams from the bushes, low hanging branches of the two trees, and the porch itself. Twice, he'd noticed Allison fidgeting on the concrete stoop. Yet, to her credit, she'd remained seated. He suspected it wasn't in her nature to force her brothers to correct their own mistakes. Or to sit idly by while they tended to chores. As firmly as she ran her business, it was obvious she had a soft spot...a blind eye...where these two were concerned.

"There," Benny said sharply. "That's the last of it."

Eric raised himself from the top step and took the three full garbage bags from Benny's grasp. "If you two want to go home and wash up and change your clothes, I thought we might all go out for pancakes. Assuming, of course, your sister approves."

"You wanna take us out for breakfast, after what we did?" Phillip asked.

He nodded. "You boys worked hard cleaning up the mess. And we have to eat. However, the decision belongs to Allison."

"Can we, Sis?" Benny asked. "You know how much we love pancakes."

She pressed her fingertips to her lips, and Eric imagined she was doing her best to suppress an outright laugh. "On one condition," she told them. "You tell me why you did this. Especially after promising you wouldn't pull a prank. And why Eric?"

Benny lowered his head, his gaze narrowed on the ground. He scuffed the dirt with the toe of his sneaker. "Just because."

Allison stepped forward until she stood in front of her brother. "That's not an answer, at least not an acceptable one."

"It's because of the way you two like each other," Phillip said. "Last week when we were helping Mr. Dunston put up his Halloween decorations, we overheard Mrs. Dunston talking about what a nice couple you two make. And then, the night you brought him his jacket, you stayed a real long time."

Tears filled Allison's eyes, the sight tightening a knot in Eric's gut. The boys were jealous.

"We're just friends, and new ones at that," Allison told them, her words twisting the knot another turn.

"I do like your sister," Eric admitted, willingly taking whatever was between them a step further. "However, there's nothing for you boys to be worried about."

"Yeah, for now," Benny grumbled. "What if you start liking each other more?"

Allison curled her fingers beneath her brother's chin and lifted, staring him straight in the eye. "More?"

Benny fidgeted at her side. Embarrassment flushed his cheeks. "You know. Like boyfriend and girlfriend. Or worse."

Eric chuckled. Memories of his own fledgling adolescence coming back to him in a rush. "What could possibly be considered 'worse', Benny?"

"Like you got married or something."

Phillip sidled up to his sister and took hold of her hand. "It'd be like when Stevie Parker's mom got married. Her new husband didn't want Stevie around so they shipped him off to live with his grandma in Ohio."

"We like Uncle David and all, but we don't want to live with him," Benny added. "He's got girls."

Phillip scrunched up his nose in disgust. "Yeah, and they're always singing and stuff. And waving their dolls in our faces. Yuk."

Eric bit back his laughter, worried his reaction might be misconstrued by the boys. They truly loved their sister, and rightfully so. And obviously, they had no intention of sharing. At least not willingly or without a fight.

Allison tugged on both boys' shirt collars, pulling them to her sides and holding them close. "You boys have nothing to worry about. I'd never, ever, send you away. No matter what happens between me and anybody."

Phillip blinked back a tear threatening release. "We love you, Sis, even if we don't always tell you."

Benny shifted in Allison's hold and turned in Eric's direction. "We're sorry about the mess we made." Raising his head, he met his sister's gaze. "And I promise...for real this time...we'll behave better. Here and at school."

Chapter Seven

Allison slid into the booth at the local pancake house, expecting Phillip to slip in at her side as he always did. Instead, he scooted onto the seat across from her, followed by Benny, leaving Eric to share her bench.

"We haven't been here in ages," she said. Snagging the menus from their spot behind the table-top jukebox, she passed them around. "I'm looking forward to a stack of their wonderful maple walnut cakes."

She studied both of her brothers across the width of the Formica table top, their noses buried in the glossy plastic menus. Her heart clenched at the thought they'd been jealous of hers and Eric's fledgling relationship.

Relationship? Isn't that a bit of a stretch?

She cast a sideways glance in Eric's direction. As if he sensed her discreet perusal, he smiled. Beneath the table, he nudged her knee with his own, and his smile split into an outright grin.

Friendship? Relationship? The idea of taking whatever this was a step further was a definite possibility.

"So," Eric said suddenly, drawing her from her thoughts. "Do you fellows like hockey?"

"You bet," Benny replied, his sharp gaze honed in on Eric across the width of the table. "I just know the Blackhawks are gonna take the cup this season."

Eric's chuckle drew Benny's frown. "Nope. Red Wings all the way."

The waitress arrived with their drinks, coffee for her and Eric and milk for the boys, interrupting their claims of hockey superiority. Once the woman left to retrieve their food order, Allison jumped into the discussion.

"Dreamers," she teased. "You're both wrong. It's going to be the Toronto Maple Leafs."

Both Benny and Eric shook their heads adamantly.

Eric shook his finger at her in mock disgust at the thought. "Never happen. The cup's not staying in Toronto. It'll either belong to Detroit, or since I live here now, I suppose I could root for the Blackhawks." He paused before adding, "In case you'd like a preview of how the season's going to go, I just happen to have four tickets for the Wings versus Blackhawks for next Friday. I don't suppose I could interest the three of you into going?"

"Wow!" Phillip chimed in, his broad grin crinkling his nose and drawing attention to his freckles. "I've never been to a real hockey game before."

"There are a few rules," Eric told them, his previous light mood shifting.

"Rules?" Benny said, gulping the word out around a mouthful of milk. "We don't do too well with rules."

Eric nodded. "So I've seen and heard. However, things can change. You boys need to think before you act. When someone eggs you on, don't respond without considering about how it's going to affect not just you, but your sister too."

Her immediate thought was to offer some sort of protest, some excuse for her brothers' repeated mistakes. Yet, in the back of her mind, she realized Eric meant no harm. No disrespect for either her or the boys. If anything, he was showing the type of support she'd been lacking, even from her older brother.

"You mean like will it make Principal Garner call her into school?" Phillip asked.

"Yes," Eric confirmed. "That's exactly what I mean. She has a business to run, filled with small children whose parents have put their trust in the fact that she'll be there for them." He sighed and shifted his gaze from one brother to the next. "Every time she has to leave to take care of something you've done, it puts undue pressure on Willa and—"

Benny cut in, laughing. "Yeah, we heard about the kid who upchucked all over you."

Eric responded with a chuckle. "He certainly did, but not on purpose. That's where the difference lies between what happened with a small child and what you boys get yourselves into. He couldn't help himself. You fellows can."

"Let me get this straight. We behave and you take us to a hockey game."

Eric nodded. "I don't believe in bribing someone to behave. However, I do feel good behavior and habits should be rewarded."

Benny nodded his head as well, echoing Eric's movement. "This could work." He turned to Allison. "What do you think, Sis?"

She waited while the waitress set their plates in front of them, along with bottles of warm syrup.

"The offer is very generous. However, I'd hate to think you're only behaving because of the promise of reward. I'd prefer you to act like young adults all the time, not just when there's a sporting event on the line."

The boys exchanged glances before Phillip admitted, "We can do that." He turned his attention to Eric. "And we are really sorry about TPing your house. We kinda like that you like our sister."

Eric nudged her thigh beneath the table and then closed his hand over hers and rested it in the space between their plates. "Good, because I kinda like her. And you fellows…you're growing on me."

The moment they arrived home, the boys shot up the stairs to their room, promising to thoroughly clean rather than just shove things beneath their bunk. Allison waited until she heard the door shut before she turned to face Eric.

"Thank you for being so great with the boys, and for breakfast."

"You're welcome." He reached out and cupped her chin in the crook of his bent finger, raising her gaze to his. "Despite the difficulties."

Her skin warmed where he touched her. Her breath caught when he caressed her lower lip with his thumb. "Difficulties?" she said softly, the telltale squeak betraying any confidence she might have had.

"You had droplets of syrup on your lips. It was all I could do to keep from leaning over and wiping them away with my tongue."

"Oh," she squeaked again. "Those kind of difficul—"

He stopped her mid-word with the press of his mouth to hers. The tip of tongue slid slowly, seductively across her lower lip.

She stood on her tiptoes and pressed her mouth to his. When he repeated the soft caress before pressing his lips more firmly to hers, her knees wobbled. Eric's strong arm anchored at her waist was the only thing that kept her standing.

Once he raised his head, he asked, "What time do the boys get picked up?"

She shifted from one foot to the other, mentally drawing herself back to reality after Eric's mind-boggling kiss.

"Uh…six…no five-thirty. David will be here at five-thirty."

"And what time will the trick or treaters start?"

"We'll have a few of the smaller ones between five and six, but the majority will come between six and nine. I usually shut the porch light off at nine-thirty."

He released the hold he'd taken at her waist and stepped back. "I'd better get moving then. I was hoping you'd want some company for the handouts, but I also have to make sure my house is covered. I wouldn't want an egging."

A quick laugh escaped her. "At least we won't have to worry about my brothers doing it." She laid her hand against his arm and scored his lightweight jacket with her fingertips. "And I'd love some company."

"Good." He pressed a chaste kiss to her cheek. "I'll be back around five-thirty, once I've got everything set up."

****

Eric shouldered the canvas bag filled with candy bars and bubble gum and crossed the street to Allison's house. He spared a backward glance at his porch, satisfied with the outcome from his afternoon trip to the hardware store and Woolworths. A small, motorized skeleton sat prominently on his top step, a bucket filled with small pieces of gum, dangling from the decoration's immobile outstretched hand. The other arm swung a wide arc and pointed toward Allison's house. The hand-decorated sign at the skeleton's feet proclaimed: *A small treat here, a bigger bite over there.*

He'd stayed put on his porch until Benny and Phillip climbed into the brown and white station wagon and the driver had pulled away.

What's the matter? Afraid to meet her big brother?

Eric shoved the taunt aside as firmly as he pushed open Allison's front gate. He had no qualms about meeting 'the family' but wanted to reach firm ground with her kid brothers before he moved on to her older sibling. At least that's what he told himself.

Yet somewhere in the back recesses of his mind, he realized he was wading into uncharted waters. Exciting waters. He'd never known anyone as self-sufficient as Allison. She wore her responsibilities like a badge of honor. While, at the same time, a sweet vulnerability simmered just beneath the surface. And, for the first time he could remember, he wanted to tap into both sides of this complicated woman.

For want of a more modern phrase, he wanted to become her knight in shining armor.

Allison answered the door almost immediately. Dressed, as she had been for the previous day's party, in a brightly colored witch's costume, she held a bowl of apples and caramels in the crook of her arm. The moment she saw him, a smile lit her comically made-up face...complete with pink-sparkled wart.

"You're here," she said, stepping back to allow him inside.

"Yes, I guess I am." He'd barely stepped across the

threshold when a group of children appeared on the porch.

"Trick or treat," the children screamed.

He spun on his heel and grinned down at a collection of witches, policemen, and even a frog. Reaching into his bag, he withdrew an assortment of chocolate bars and tossed one into each child's sack. Allison followed suit, giving each child an apple and caramel.

"You know," she said the moment the children had left, "the older ones will try to sneak back in hopes of another chocolate bar."

A deep, throaty laugh escaped him. "I'd accounted for the possibility. I know I did the same when I was a kid." He leaned in her direction, peering into her bowl of treats. "Not so much for the apples though."

"Their parents will thank me."

He withdrew a chocolate bar from his bag and waved it in front of her. "Maybe. But the kids will like me more."

Allison snatched the candy from his hand. "Umm...mallow cups...my favorite."

"Mine too." Taking a second bar from his bag, he tore the wrapper open. "It makes me wonder what else we might have in common."

Any hope of holding an in-depth discussion with Allison over the course of the next couple of hours was a waste. Steady streams of trick-or-treaters ascended and descended the stairs one after the other. And as Allison had predicted, there were repeats.

"Isn't it nine-thirty yet?" he asked, rummaging through what little remained of the treats he'd purchased.

"Almost." She pressed a hand to his shoulder. "If you think you can hold down the fort alone for a few minutes, I'll go make a pot of tea." She took a few steps toward the kitchen, but then stopped to ask, "Unless you'd rather have wine."

He shook his head. "Tea is fine. Especially if you have some choco-blast cookies to go with it."

She nodded slightly toward the crumpled wrappers on the entryway table. "Something tells me we've both had enough chocolate. How about a raspberry scone instead?"

"Spoilsport."

The sound of Allison's laughter as she went down the hallway toward the kitchen wrapped around him like a warm and welcome blanket.

Chapter Eight

Allison wrapped her hands around the steaming mug of tea and settled back into the thickly upholstered chair in her living room. Eric sat opposite her on the matching sofa.

"Thank you for keeping me company this evening."

Eric looked up from his tea and smiled. "My pleasure."

His smile, his softly worded answer, sent an unaccustomed awareness skittering across the very surface of her skin. Her pulse picked up speed. "Can I get you more tea?"

"No." He raised his hand, crooked his finger, and motioned for her to join him on the sofa. "I'd much rather have a kiss."

She pushed herself to her feet slowly, testing her ability to walk on legs that suddenly felt like jelly. "A kiss would be good." She took a seat at Eric's side and melted into his arms. When she raised her head and met his gaze, she admitted, "Maybe the kiss will lead to something even better."

His kiss was a heady mixture of sweet and steamy and even better than she remembered. He maneuvered his way from chaste, to wet, to hot, with the finesse of someone far more experienced than she. Happily lost in his kiss, it was a moment or two before she realized he'd taken a death grip on the hem of her sweater, the tug on the soft material evident each time his fingers flexed. He was obviously holding himself in check, no doubt to keep her from bolting as she'd done the first time they'd kissed.

She released the grasp she'd taken on Eric's forearms and circled his wrist with her fingers. Tentatively, on the off chance she was reading him wrong, she eased his hand beneath the hem of her sweater and guided him upward across her midriff.

The moment he wrapped his hand around her satin-covered breast, she trembled. The slow, deliberate pass of his thumb across her nipple sent a jolt of electricity coursing through her entire body, settling with pinpoint accuracy on the tightened crest.

A gasp slipped past her lips. "Oh...my." A second stroke of his thumb sent her squirming in his arms.

He pressed his mouth to hers, nipping at her lower lip until she opened for him, allowing him the access he requested. In slow, deliberate increments, he slid his tongue across hers, deepening the kiss. Beneath her sweater, he dusted his fingertips across her chest and took possession of her opposite breast. And as he'd done to the first, he coaxed the crest into pebbled hardness through the thin satin covering.

She needed the feel of his bare hand against her skin as surely as she needed another stroke of his tongue, another taste of the herbal tea and fruity scone fed to her with his kiss. Boldly, she gathered the hem of her sweater in her hand and pushed it upward, reveling in the feel of the air against her bare midriff.

"Are you sure?" he whispered, his lips skimming hers as he spoke.

She nodded. "Yes, I'm positive."

He sighed deeply, his warm breath washing over her face. He slid his fingertips beneath the edge of her bra and stroked her stiff nipple. With the slightest of tugs, he pulled the lace-edged cup aside, baring her for his gaze.

Her skin tingled. When he bent his head and took the very tip of her breast in his mouth, she shamelessly arched into him.

He moved from one breast to the other, stroking, sucking, teasing her with both his hands and mouth. When he'd coaxed the very breath from her lungs, he released her and pressed his forehead to her chest. "I'm going crazy here," he admitted. "I want more. I want it all, but only if that's what you want too."

"Yes," she said, her voice rough with desire. "Please."

Eric rose from the sofa and lifted her into his arms. "Which way?"

Allison pulled in a ragged breath, gave less than a second's thought to what they were about to do, and told him, "Down the hall, first door on the left."

****

Eric awoke the early the next morning amid a pile of rumpled sheets and fluffy pink comforter. It took a moment or two before the fog cleared and he realized he's spent the night in Allison's bed.

And what a night it had been.

Mental note number five: on the off chance this wasn't a fluke, a quick trip to the drugstore is in order.

The pungent aroma of freshly brewed coffee drew him from beneath the covers and toward the small, attached bath. A quick shower and mouthful of

Listerine and he'd be ready to coax Allison back to bed. He thought of retrieving his clothes from their scattered position across the bedroom floor but opted instead for a large bath towel wrapped around his waist. Hopefully, the easy access would entice her to continue what they'd started the night before.

Less than ten minutes later, he found her in the kitchen, her attention given to the food items she'd laid out on the countertop. Dressed in little more than a long t-shirt that barely covered the rounded curve of her bare bottom, she had him instantly aroused. Within a heartbeat, he was standing at her back, his lips pressed against the smooth slope of her throat. "Good morning, beautiful."

She arched her neck, offering him unfettered access to her silky skin. "Good morning to you too."

"How long have you been up?" Given they'd not fallen asleep until halfway through the night, he'd been surprised when he'd woken up alone.

"Since seven, and that's an hour later than usual."

"I wore you out, did I?" he teased.

"Given it's now eight-thirty, I'm guessing it was me who did the wearing out, not the other way around."

He wrapped his arms around her waist and pulled her back against the beginnings of another arousal. "You were delightfully insatiable, I do have to admit."

She shifted against him, taunting him with her luscious curves. "And you were just as delightfully accommodating."

"How about we forget breakfast and head back to the bedroom?" He made a show of scanning the entire room. "Or we could stay here for a pre-breakfast quickie."

She turned in his arms and pressed her soft, pouty lips to his. When he opened his mouth, she slid her tongue into place and deepened what promised to be a perfect kiss. He returned the wet intrusion with one of his own, trading tastes seamlessly between short, staccato gasps for air.

She was driving him deliciously mad, and he loved every minute of it.

Eric pulled her tightly against his body, letting her know in no uncertain terms how badly he wanted her. Anchoring his hands beneath her hips, he lifted her off her feet, and coaxed her to wrap her legs around his waist.

With a sharp tug on the edge of the towel, he stripped the terry cloth from between them until they were skin against skin. In turn, she wrestled the cotton shirt off over her head. Her creamy breasts pressed firmly to his chest. One shift of his hips and he'd be inside her.

"Not here," she whispered against the side of his throat.

He took her mouth in another deep, wet kiss and then carried her the short distance to the bedroom, managing to reach the bed without incident despite the array of clothing items scattered across the floor. With what little restraint he could manage, he tore open the last of the foil packets, and followed Allison down into the depths of the big four-poster bed.

Mental note number six: the next time we come for air, remember to tell her it's not just sex and that you've fallen in love.

Epilogue

Six Months Later

Allison withdrew the last batch of choco-blast cookies from the oven and set the tray on the counter to cool. With Eric and her brothers out for the evening, she'd spent the past few hours baking and thinking.

The past half a year had been absolutely wonderful. The best of her adult life. Eric had endeared himself to her brothers, not just with hockey games or trips to restaurants, but in the way he'd cautiously insinuated himself into their lives.

He'd shown them he cared. He'd listened to their adolescent rants and offered good advice. He'd even signed up to coach Benny's little league team and taken Phillip to the YMCA and taught him to swim. Above all, he'd given her the support and encouragement she'd been lacking. He'd lifted the burden of responsibility from her shoulders and offered to share the weight.

His ad agency was booming, yet he always made time for all of them. Whether it was a sporting event, a trip to The Field Museum, or just a night gathered in front of Eric's fancy color television, they'd become a family.

Lost in her thoughts, it was a moment or two before she realized she wasn't alone.

"You're home early." Drawn to the sight of Eric

standing in her kitchen doorway, she removed her apron and wiped her damp hands on the closest tea towel. "How'd the game go?"

"The Blackhawks won. Now we go back to Montreal for the seventh game."

Eric pulled her into his arms and, as easily as the chocolate chips in her cookies, she melted into his embrace. "Benny must be excited."

"Tell me about it. He kept reminding me that he was right and we were wrong." He chuckled. "I think David was about ready to string him up from the rafters by the end of the night."

"It was nice of you to invite David to the game. I'm glad the two of you have hit it off."

He shrugged, the lift and fall of his broad shoulders pulling her attention to his nicely toned body. "What can I say? I'm likeable."

She raised her head and pressed a chaste kiss to his lips. "That you are."

"Besides, in less than three months, I'll be his brother-in-law, and he'll be stuck with me. He might as well get used to me now."

"You're an easy fellow to get used to. I managed it in no time at all."

He returned her previous kiss with a similar one. Chaste, non-committal. "The boys went home with David for the night, so we've got the house to ourselves. If you're interested, I'd be happy to show you another, more inventive, side of my personality."

She shot him a smile and batted her eyelashes in a teasing fashion. "More inventive than whipped cream and chocolate sauce? How about our tryst in your backyard hammock?"

"My imagination hasn't even left the starting gate."

"Hmm. Sounds interesting."

Eric took her hand in his and coaxed her down the hallway, past her bedroom door, and out onto the enclosed sun porch. Once he'd seated them both on the cushioned chaise, he reached for the hem of her blouse and drew the soft cotton over her head.

"This seems like a good place," he mumbled, his lips pressed against the bare skin above the edge of her bra. With the flick of his fingers, he loosened the catch and stripped the scrap of silk and lace slowly, seductively from her body. Her breasts fell into his waiting hands.

The late-April breeze seeped through the louvered windows. It was dark both outside and within the confines of the sunroom. She knew they were all but invisible to prying eyes, yet there was a definite decadence to making love somewhere so open. A nervous excitement settled in the pit of her stomach. The same excitement she felt every time they made love.

"I love you," she whispered.

His hands stilled against her skin. He pressed a feather-light kiss to her midriff then lifted his head. "I love you, too." He paused, pressed a second kiss to the same spot, and then added, "And if it takes me the rest of my life, I going to prove it to you over and over again."

Allison's Choco-blast Cookies

Ingredients:
1 cup butter, softened
1 ½ cups white sugar
2 large eggs
2 teaspoons pure vanilla extract
2 cups all-purpose flour
2/3 cup cocoa powder
¾ teaspoon baking soda
¼ teaspoon sale
1 cup semisweet chocolate chips
1 cup milk chocolate chips
½ cup chopped pecans

Directions:
Preheat oven to 350 degrees

In large bowl, beat butter, sugar, eggs and vanilla until light and fluffy.

In a separate bowl combine flour, cocoa, baking soda and salt. Add into butter mixture in four parts, stirring completely after each addition. Mix in chips and pecans and give one final stir.

Drop by teaspoonful onto ungreased cookie sheets.

Bake 8 to 10 minutes or just until set. Cool slightly on the cookie sheet before transferring to wire racks to cool completely.

Makes 4 dozen cookies. Or, if you're like Allison, 3 dozen *larger* cookies!

A word about the author...

Like most authors, Nancy began writing at an early age, usually on the walls and with crayons or, heaven forbid, permanent markers. Her love of writing often made her the English teacher's pet which, of course, resulted in a whole lot of teasing. Still, it was worth it.

When not writing, Nancy dotes on her five grandchildren and enjoys reading and travel. She lives in Atlantic Canada, where she enjoys the beautiful scenery and colorful people.

Please feel free to visit her website at www.nancyfraser.ca, like her on Facebook, or follow her on Twitter @nfraserauthor. Or just enjoy what she writes.

Thank you for purchasing
this publication of The Wild Rose Press, Inc.

If you enjoyed the story, we would appreciate your
letting others know by leaving a review.

For other wonderful stories,
please visit our on-line bookstore at
www.thewildrosepress.com.

For questions or more information
contact us at
info@thewildrosepress.com.

The Wild Rose Press, Inc.
www.thewildrosepress.com

Stay current with The Wild Rose Press, Inc.

Like us on Facebook

https://www.facebook.com/TheWildRosePress

And Follow us on Twitter
https://twitter.com/WildRosePress

Only Yours
by Nancy Fraser
https://amzn.com/B019YI0YYA

Everyone expects Rebecca Winston to marry her high school/college sweetheart, Garrett Langley. The problem is, the flame's gone out on their romance. They're still best of friends, but only friends. When Garrett's father has a heart attack, his older brother Wyatt (an L.A. attorney) returns home for the first time in years. The attraction between Rebecca and Wyatt is immediate.

Can Rebecca expect her family and, especially, Garrett to understand that her desires have changed and turned toward Wyatt?

Can Wyatt get past the feeling that he's poaching his younger brother's girl?

Also Available
Pumpkinnapper
by Linda Banche
https://amzn.com/B0056H27R6

Pumpkin thieves, a youthful love rekindled, and a jealous goose. Oh my!

Last night someone tried to steal the widowed Mrs. Emily Metcalfe's pumpkins. She's certain the culprit is her old childhood nemesis and the secret love of her youth, whom she hasn't seen in ten years.

Henry, Baron Grey has never forgotten the girl he loved, but couldn't pursue, and so decides to catch Emily's would-be thief. Even after she reveals his childhood nickname--the one he would rather forget. And even after her jealous pet goose bites him in an embarrassing place.

Oh, the things a man will do for love.